The Lovers Assistant; Or, New Art of Love

By Henry Fielding

NATAL PUBLISHING LLC
ARS LONGA, VITA BREVIS

PREFACE

This Work was begun many Years ago, though altered in some Places by the Author, before his Death; as will appear by the modern Instances introduced in it. Many of which being so applicable to the present Time, is the Occasion of it being now published.

As to any Exception which may be made to the Impurity of this Work, we shall transcribe what was written long ago in its Defence, from the Preface prefixed to Mr. Dryden*'s Translation of this Poem.*

'A great many People are mistaken in these Books; and tho' they were made use of as a Pretence to drive the Author from the Court of *Augustus*, and confine him to *Tomos* on the Frontiers of the *Getae* and *Sarmatae*, yet they were not the true Cause of his Confinement. They are very far from being so licentious as the Writings of several other Poets, both *Greek* and *Latin*. However we must own he might have been a little more discreet, especially in some Places[A].

[Note A: He means in the other two Books.]

'That which offended the *Romans* most in this Work, cannot touch us. It has always been more dangerous in *Italy* to converse with Women of Honour, and frequent their Houses, than 'tis with us; where there is more Liberty, and what in that Country may be an Occasion of Debauchery, would not at all be so in ours.

'Notwithstanding all that has been said against these Books *of the Art of Love*, by some over-scrupulous Persons, whose Discretion has too much of Affectation in it: they are not only necessary for the Knowledge of the *Latin* Tongue, and the *Roman* History, concerning which they contain several Things very particular; but for the noble Sentiments we find in them, which the *Gravest* and *Learnedest* Writers have thought worthy to be quoted for *Authorities*.

'In a Word, there's nothing in them that comes near the *Licence* of some *Epigrams* of *Catullus, Martial*, and *Ausonius*, of some *Satires* of *Horace* and *Juvenal*, and several other Pieces of *Ancient* and *Modern* Authors, which are read and commented upon; and about which even celebrated *Jesuits* and other religious Persons, as eminent for their Piety as their Erudition, have employed their Studies. Yet who has condemn'd or complain'd of them? We must confess, such Things should be managed with Address; and those of them who have meddled with any of the Authors I have named, have shewn that it may be done so, by their succeeding so happily in it.

'As for this Treatise of the *Art of Love*, for which the Author has also prescrib'd a *Remedy*, as it is liable to be ill interpreted by those whose Pens poison every Thing they touch; so it may bear a good Construction, by such as know how to turn every Thing to Advantage.

'I will yet say, this *Art* may be apply'd to those that intend to marry. There is nothing sure against Decency in all that. I agree, if you will have it so, that it extends so far as to direct one to the Means to gain a Mistress. If this was not lawful heretofore in *Italy*, on account of the jealous Humour of the *Italians*, we cannot, for the same Reason only, say it ought to be forbidden in our Country, any more than in several others, provided we could be sure the Ladies Modesty would not be offended, before whom Youth should be always careful not to exceed the Bounds of the Respect that's due to them.'

To this I may add, that if the Objection of Impurity lies against any Part of this Work, it is only against the two latter Books, for in that which we have here paraphrased, there is nothing capable of offending the nicest Ear.

With regard to the Merit of this Paraphrase, which is entirely a new Undertaking, and might perhaps, if properly encouraged, be carried on with other Latin Poets, we shall only observe, that the utmost Care hath been taken to preserve the Spirit and true Sense of the

Author, and where we have been obliged to deviate, we have given the literal Translation in the Notes.

Upon the whole, we cannot suppress, what one of the most learned Men of this Age, said upon persuing the Paraphrase, viz. That he thought it would serve better to explain the Meaning of *Ovid* to a Learner, than any other Translation, or all his numerous Commentators.

BOOK I

If in so learned an Age as this, when Arts and Sciences are risen to such Perfection, there be any Gentleman unskilled in the Art of Loving, let him come to my School; where, if he hath any Genius, he will soon become an Adept: For I would by no means have any young Gentlemen think, that Erudition is unnecessary upon this Occasion. It is well known that the [1]Rules of Art are necessary to the Conduct of a Ship; for which reason, none but able and experienced Seamen are preferred to the Command of one. Rules are necessary even to make a good Coachman, as those Gentlemen who have the Ambition to excel this way very well know. In the same manner is Art required to drive the Chariot of Love well. Now it hath pleased *Venus* to place me in the Coach-Box: what a Captain is to a Ship, or the Driver to his Chariot, that am I to Love. I own indeed Master *Cupid* is a little wild, and often stubborn; but he is only a Child, and of an Age to be disciplined: And however fierce the Disposition of a Lad may be, a judicious Schoolmaster knows very well how to correct it: For many a Boy who hath afterwards turned out a Hero, hath when at School very patiently submitted to the Lash, and quietly, at the Word of Command, held out his Hands to be whipt [2]. Duke *William* [3] himself, when a Lad, very possibly submitted to Correction; and he [4] who was hereafter to become the Terror of his Enemies, might in his Youth have been afraid of his Tutor. Mr. *Pointz* was his Preceptor: I am the Preceptor of Love. Both these Youths were of a fierce Disposition, both elevated [5] in their Birth. But as the stoutest Ox submits himself to the Yoke, and the most fiery Horse to the Bridle, so shall Love to me. Though he may bend his Bow against my Breast, and shake his Torches at me; no matter: nay, the more he pierces me with his Arrows, the more he burns me, the more severely will I be revenged of him.

But here, Master *Apollo*, I will tell no lies to my Readers. I do not pretend to have received any Inspiration from you, any more than from Parson *Whitefield* [6]: And as for Miss *Clio* [7] and her eight Sisters, I never visit them; nor have I even a Cap-Acquaintance with them. I write from Experience only; and *Experto crede Roberto* is my Motto. I promise my Readers that I will tell them truth; and if I must, for form sake, invoke any Muse, *Venus* herself shall be the Person [8]. Sweet Goddess! then be thou present, and smile at my

Undertaking. But as for you who cannot smile, I mean you, Prudes, with your screw'd Faces, which may be considered as Signs hung forth before the Door of Virtue, and which perhaps, like other Signs, promise what is not to be found in the House; I desire neither your Favour nor your Company. Good-natur'd Girls[9] are all I write to; and such I promise them may read my Works without a Blush.

Know then, my good Scholar, that art unexperienced in the Art of Love, that this Art consists of three principal Points: First, to select a proper Mistress: Secondly, to win her Affections: And, Thirdly, to preserve your mutual Affection. Of all these therefore we will treat; or, to speak metaphorically, through these three Roads we will drive the Chariot we have undertaken to guide.

First then as to the Choice of a Mistress, to whom you may say, *In Thee alone my choice is fixed.* Do not believe such a one will fall into your Lap. It will become you to look about sharp for her, and with all your Eyes, I do assure you. And here my first Instruction shall be, where she may most probably be found: For he is a bad Huntsman who would beat about the *Royal Exchange* for a Hare or a Fox; and not a much better Gunner or Fisherman, who goes a shooting in *Somerset-Gardens*, or attempts to angle in the magnificent Bason there. As these all know the Places where their Game resort, so must you.

Here then, I by no means advise you to make a long Voyage after a foreign Mistress, as *Perseus* did, who fetched *Andromeda*[10] from the *Indies*; or *Paris*, whom nothing would serve but a *Grecian* Mistress. Your own Country, my Friend, will produce Women which the World cannot equal. Beauties are as plenty in the City of *London* as Apples in[11] *Herefordshire*, or Grains of Wheat[12] in *Hampshire*; they are indeed as plenty as Fish in the Sea, or Birds in the Air; nay, the Sky hath not more Stars than *London* hath Beauties: for *England*[13], not *Cyprus*, is the Queen of Love's favourite Island. Whether you love green Fruit, and which is in the Bud only, or Beauty in its fuller Bloom, or that which is arrived to perfect Ripeness; nay, if nothing but Wisdom or Sagacity will serve your turn, of these too Old *England* will afford you a sufficient Plenty.

In the pleasant Month of *May*, repair to *Vaux-Hall*[14]. Here take your Evening Walk, either round the verdant Scenes, where Nightingales, the only Foreigners who give us their Songs for nothing, warble their most delicious Notes. When your Limbs demand Repose, you may enjoy it in an Alcove, from whence the embattel'd Troops

of *Venus* will pass in review before you. Again, the lofty Dome of *Ranelagh* invites your Steps. Whether the illustrious Artist took his Model from that House, which as a Reward for their Industry, or for some little regard for their Honey, the benevolent Nature of Man hath conferred on that laborious Animal the Bee: Or whether a more pious Disposition chose this Form from the musical Instrument which summons the whole Parish to Church: Or whether the wondrous Force of Genius, unassisted by any Model, did not of itself strike out this wondrous Architecture; let *Kent* or *Benson* inquire. Hither, from every Corner of the Town, repair the loveliest Nymphs. Here too thou may'st survey them, either walking or reposed on Benches at thy Ease. Nor is the *Mall* to be neglected, where once die brawny Arm of *Charles* displayed its Strength, and beat his subtle Courtiers at the Play, whence it derives its Name. Nor, *Kensington*, must thy Gardens be passed by, once the Delight of mighty *Caroline*, and to the future Age a Monument of her Taste. Here the Charmers draw in sweet Air, and send it forth again in sweeter Sighs, as Tributes to the loved Memory of that mighty Queen. As for the Ring, formerly the Scene of Beauty's many Triumphs, it is now become a lonely deserted Place: Brilliants and brilliant Eyes no longer sparkle there: No more the heedless Beau falls by the random Glance, or well-pointed Fan. The Ring is now no more: Yet *Ruckholt*, *Marybone* and *The Wells* survive; Places by no means to be neglected by the Gallant: for Beauty may lurk beneath the Straw Hat, and *Venus* often clothes her lovely Limbs in Stuffs. Nay, the very Courts of Law are not excluded; and the Scenes of Wrangling are sometimes the Scenes of Love. In that Hall where *Thames* sometimes overflowing, washes the Temple of *Venus Lucy*, the grave Serjeant becomes a Victim to the Fair; and he who so well knows how to defend others, cannot defend himself. Here the Special Pleader loses all Power to Demurr, and finds beyond his Expectation a novel Assignment spring up in the Cause. Him *Venus Lucy*[15] laughs at from her neighbouring Temple; for the Council is now become the Client, and squeezes an empty Hand harder than he ever did a full one. But above all, the Theatres are the Place of Sport: for these will be most fruitful to your Wishes. Here you will find one Object to love, and another to toy with. Some, of whom a single Touch will suffice, and others, in whom you will desire a stronger Tenure. Neither do the Ants in pursuit of Grain, or the Bees in quest of Flowers, swarm in greater Numbers than the Beauties to the Theatres. The variety of Charmers here

have often distracted my Choice. Hither they come to see, and to be themselves seen; and many are the Love-Bargains here made.

And now, Friend, I will tell you a Story. *Romulus* was the first Person who ever made this use of the Theatre, when he ordered his Soldiers to fall foul on the *Sabine* Ladies, whom he invited to a Play acted by his

Command. Not that I would have you think, that Theatre was like the Playhouse in *Convent-Garden*, enriched with Scenes, Machines, and other Decorations. To say the truth, it was no better than a Barn, or Booth. Here he assembled the *Sabine* Girls, and ordered his *Romans* to chuse every Man his Miss. They did so, and while the poor Girls thought no Harm, those Fellows felt strange Emotions within. Now while a certain Dancer, called, *The Ludio*, was performing *a Tambourine*, which I suppose took greatly at that time, *Romulus* on a sudden gave the Signal for falling on. This was instantly obeyed. They all rushed in, laid their Hands upon the Girls, and soon gave them sufficient Tokens of their Purpose.

As the Doves, who are the most timorous of Birds, fly from Eagles; or as the young Lamb runs from Wolves, as soon as she sees them, so terrified were these Ladies, at the Men rushing upon them, in this unlawful manner. The Colour forsook their Cheeks at once. All were equally in a Fright, though they discovered their Fear by different Symptoms. Some of them tear their Hair, others sit in Amazement, Terror strikes some dumb, others call in vain for the Assistance of their Mammas. One cries out, another is shocked to death; one stands still, another endeavours to get out of the House. But all their Endeavours are vain; and perhaps indeed their Blushes heightened their Beauty; they were all led off, and those who would not go were carried. Methinks, I hear one of their Gallants thus addressing his weeping Fair. *Why, my Dear, will you spoil those lovely Eyes with Tears? I promise you, you shall be served no worse than your Mother hath been before. I will only do to you, what your Father did to her.* Ah *Romulus! Romulus!* no General ever better knew how to reward his Soldiers; I promise you, that when I hear your Drum beating up for Voluntiers, I will enlist under your Command.

Ever since that time, the Theatre hath been consecrated to Love, and many a pretty Girl, since the *Sabines*, hath owed the Loss of her Maidenhead to it.

Other Places of publick Meeting may likewise be frequented, as Horse Races[16] and the Like. And especially public Shews, which never fail of Women. Here get upon a crouded Scaffold, and sit next

to the Girl you like. Squeeze yourself as close to her as you can; for Custom here countenances such squeezing whether the pretty Creatures will or no. Here find some Opportunity to begin a Discourse; you will not be driven to talk upon your Fingers, or by Signs, but may use your Tongue[B]. Begin then with News, or the Chitchat of the Town. Nay, the Shew itself will afford a Subject: for instance supposing it was my Lord

Mayor's Shew, you may ask her what Alderman that Coach, or those Liveries belong to; and be sure to admire the same with herself: Do not omit moreover, to give her an early Intimation of your Gallantry, and that you are a Woman's Man. If it should happen that any one of the Aldermen should be a greater Cuckold than the rest of his Brethren; take care to titter at his Appearance; and while the Pageants[17] are passing by, endeavour to find out a Resemblance of Horns in some of them. All those Things have a remote Tendency to this great point.

[Note B: These Verses are transposed from the Place in which they stand in the Original, and this, I think, with Advantage to the Connection.]

If a Grain of Snuff should happen to fall on the Lady's Bosom, wipe it off with your Fingers; and if none fall, wipe off that none. Take every Opportunity to be as officious in her Service as possible. If she drop her Fan or Gloves, presently take them up; for this you will have sure Reward in the very Fact, for you may at the same time lift up her petticoat and see her Legs.

Be careful that the Person who sits behind her doth not press her tender Back with his Knee. Small Matters captivate light Minds. Many a Man hath drawn considerable Advantage from handing[18] a Lady to Coach, by gallanting her Fan, or even by taking up her Clog[19].

Nor will[20] *Tower-hill*, when the Tragic Scaffold is strewed with Saw-Dust, be an improper Place to begin your Intrigue: for *Cupid* himself always attends, and acts the Part of an Executioner on such Occasions; many a poor Man having lost his Heart, while he hath attended to another's losing his Head. While the Fair-One carelessly laying her Hand on his, argues concerning the Criminal's Guilt, and offers to lay a Wager that he will die well; the wounded Lover feels a sudden Stroke, and is not better able to bear the Smart without a Sigh.

[21]If it was the Custom of *England* to imitate the *Romans* in insulting over the Conquered, what Spectacles might have formerly been exhibited! How many *French* Youths and Virgins might have followed

the Chariot-Wheels of our Monarchs! In that Cafe many a poor *English* Heart must have submitted to a *French* Conquest, and Beauty would have been triumphant in Chains. Nay, I prophesy we shall again see those victorious Times. Our Mighty GEORGE now meditates new Triumphs, and *France*[22] shall be punished as she ought. Rejoice, O ye Shades[23], whose Bodies lie buried in the Plains of *Fontenoy*, where *British* Colours were polluted by *Gallic* Hands. WILLIAM your Avenger comes. The General in him shone forth in his first Campaign, and while a Youth, he managed War beyond his Years. Let not his Age therefore deter us from ranking him among our greatest Commanders. His Warlike Genius springs forth and outruns his Years, impatient of the sluggish Pace of Time. The *Swedish Charles*[24] was scarce beyond a Child when he crushed two mighty enemies at once; *Charles*[25] the *German* Prince, yet but a Youth, what was he when he past the *Rhine* and terrified the Host of *France*? Thy Father's Genius, WILLIAM, and his Courage, shall inspire thy youthful Arms. With that Genius and that Courage shalt thou conquer. Such Beginnings dost thou owe to the mighty Name of thy illustrious Sire; that thou who art the Noblest of all young Commanders mayst hereafter become the first among the old. 'Tis time to avenge the Injuries attempted to thy House, and to maintain thy glorious Father's Rights. Thy Country's Father and thy own, girts on thy Sword, and thy Cause is no less glorious than thy Arms. In both is *France* inferiour, and to both shall yield. I prophesy, that thou shalt conquer, and to thy Conquest I dedicate my votive Prayers, prepared hereafter to resound thy Praise; when we shall see thee, most lovely Prince, returning, thy Glories far outshining the Gold in which thou art attired. Thee shall Crouds of Youths and beauteous Virgins hail from their crouded Windows as thou passest, and universal Joy shall overspread each *British* Face on that Blest Day.

If then, my Scholar, thou shouldst happen to be placed in a Window near some lovely Girl, who, fired with the Glories of the young Conqueror, should enquire into all his matchless Labours[26], his Wound at *Dettingen*; his Danger and Intrepidity at *Fontenoy*; his Toils at home, in defiance of Cold and Fatigue; his Pursuit to *Carlisle*; his Victory at *Culloden*; and many more which will then be as well known; repeat all if thou canst, and if thy Memory fails, go on nevertheless: for Invention cannot here outdo the Reality, and thy Fictions shall recommend thee equal with Truth to her Ears.

Again, when thou dost sit down at table among the Women, thou may'st reap other Pleasures besides those of Wine: For, to speak figuratively, *Cupid* with glowing Cheeks often presses the Horns of *Bacchus* in his tender Arms; and the Wings of the little God of Love being wetted with Wine, he is unable to fly off: And if he happens to shake his wet Wings, he may possibly sprinkle the Bosom of your Mistress with Love.

In more intelligible Language, Wine fills our Minds with Courage, and makes them susceptible of other warm Passions. Care flies away, and is dissolved in much Liquor. Then comes Laughter, the poor Man becomes bold, and Grief and Solicitude, and knitted Brows vanish. Then it is that

Simplicity, a rare Virtue in our Age, opens our Hearts, Wine having divested us of Cunning. At this Season, many a watchful young Fellow hath gained the Heart of his Mistress[27]. And Love hath sprung from Wine, as the Flame doth from Fire.

However, do not confide too much at this time to the Light of a Candle: for Night and Wine obstruct us in forming a true Judgment of Beauty. *Paris* beheld the Goddesses in open Daylight, when he gave the Preference to *Venus*. Indeed by Candle-light, and in a Side-Box, almost every one is a Beauty: Jewels, Clothes, and Women, are all best discerned by the Light of the Sun.

And here if I should recount all the rural Haunts in which a Lover may find his Game, I might write more Volumes than *Oldmixon*, *Tunbridge*, and *Scarborough*, and *Cheltenham*, and *Holt*, and many other Places shall be therefore omitted; but, Bath[28], thy sulphurous Waters must not be past by. Hence Master *Dapperwit* bringing home the Wounds made by fair Eyes in his Bosom, cries out, on his Return, *The Waters are not so wholesome as they are reported; I have received more Harm than Good at the Place*.

Here rises the Temple[29] of the God (CNASH) whose Walls are hung round with the Portraits of Beauties. The Apotheosis of this God hath cost many a poor Man his Heart.

Thus far, my Scholar, I have endeavoured to instruct thee in what Places thou art to hunt for thy Game, and where to spread thy Net. I will now proceed to shew thee by what Means Puss is to be taken, when you have found her Sitting.

Mind all, as my old Schoolmaster used to say; for I assure you my instructions will be worthy the Attention of both the Great Vulgar and the Small.

My first Lesson then is: Be confident. Believe every Woman is to be come at. Do but spread your Net, and I warrant she runs into it.

Sooner shall the Birds be silent in the Spring, or the Frogs in the Winter: Sooner shall the Greyhound run away from the Hare, than a Woman shall resist the Youth who gently assails her. Though she skrews up her Face ever so demurely, she will at length yield to his Persuasions.

A dark Corner is as agreeable to a Girl, as to one of us, though we cannot so well dissemble our Desires as she can; but if we should once enter into a Confederacy against the Sex to leave off courting them, they would soon begin to act the Part of Lovers, and come a wooing to us.

And what is this but a natural Affection, common to the Females of every other Species, who often make love to the Males? And give me leave to tell the Ladies, that we are more able to command our Affections, nor are our Desires so furious, and exceeding all Bounds, as theirs.

The Story of *Byblis*[30] is too well known to be related, who being in love with her Brother, punished her Crime with her own Hands, and hanged herself in her Garters.

Miss *Myrrha*[31] loved her Papa with an Affection improper for a Daughter; for which she was turned into a Tree. I do assure you the Story is true; and the Tree now drops continual Tears for her Offence, which we use as a Perfume; and they retain the Lady's Name.

In the shady Valleys of *Ida*[32], there was a white Bull, which was the Glory of the Farmer to whom he belonged. This Bull had a beautiful black Speck between his Horns, all the rest of his Body being as white as Milk. With him the *Gnossian* and *Cydonian* Heifers were all in love, and eagerly longed to be embraced by him in the tenderest manner in which Bulls embrace the Fair Sex of Cows. *Pasiphaë*, I am very sorry to say it, conceived a Passion worse, if possible, than that of Mrs. *Mary Hamilton*, for this Bull. Lady —— is not more envied in the Drawing-Room than was every handsome Heifer by this unfortunate Woman. The Story is so well known that there is not a Freethinker[33] in the Age who can refuse his Credit to it, though they believe nothing which they cannot see and account for. This poor Girl is reported to have mowed the sweetest Grass with her own Hands for her beloved Bull. She likewise wandered

about among the Cows, without the least Regard to Mr. Alderman. *Minos* her Husband; for a Bull had totally supplanted him in her Esteem. Alas! *Pasiphaë*, to what purpose are the brocaded Petticoats? Your Gallant is not sensible of your Finery. Why do you consult your Looking-Glass, in order to pursue the Mountain-Herds? Or why with so much Art do you set your *Tête*? If you will consult your Glass, let it inform you you are no Heifer. Ah! how desirous are you to have those Horns on your own Forehead, which you intend to graft on your Husband's! It would be better to preserve your Virtue, and be constant to the Alderman, if you can like him: But if you must make a Cuckold of him, do it at least with a young Fellow. No; nothing but a Bull will suffice. She leaves the Alderman's House, and flies away to the Groves and Mountains. To say the truth, I believe she used to drink away her Senses; and that is the best Excuse for her. Ah! how often hath she cast a jealous Eye on some Heifer! and cried out, *Why should that vixen please my Love? Behold, says she, how the Slut dances a Minuet on the Grass before him: Let me die, but she is silly enough to think her Airs become her in my Love's Eyes.* At length she resolved to punish her Rivals. One Heifer she ordered barbarously to be yoked to the Plough; another she condemned to be sacrificed, and held the Entrails of the poor Victim in her Hand with all the insulting Triumph of a Rival: *Now*, says she, having the Entrails in her Hand, *now go and make yourself agreeable to my Dear*. At one time she wishes to be *Europa*[34], at another *Io*: for one of these was herself the Wife of a Bull, and the other made her Horse of one.

Filled with these Thoughts, she contrived the strangest Method of compleating her Desires. She sent for a Joiner of great Ingenuity, and ordered him to make her a large Cow of Wood. Into this she conveyed herself, and thus deceived Master Bull into her Embraces.

She conceived by this monstrous Coition, and brought forth an Offspring, which by his partaking equally of the human and taurine Form, betrayed her horrid Passion.

If the *Cretan* Lady[35] had abstained from the Love of *Thyestes*, (O! how Women disdain Constancy to their Husbands!) the Sun had not stopt in the middle of his Career, and turned about his Face to the East, that he might avoid the bloody Banquet. God be praised! the Cuckolds of our Age are not so bloody in their Revenge.

The Daughter of *Nisus*[36], who stole her Papa's Hair, feeds hungry Dogs in those Parts which first set her a longing for *Minos*.

Agamemnon, after returning safe from so many bloody Campaigns, and from the dangerous Seas which he crossed, fell at last a dreadful Victim to the Whore his Wife[37].

Who hath not wept at the sad Story of *Creüsa*? consumed by the Flames of a Sorceress, who afterwards drenched her Hands in the Blood of her own Children[38].

Phoenix[39], the Son of *Amyntor*, hath often paid many a Tear for his Amours, though he had not the wretched Fate of *Hippolytus*[40], to be torn in pieces by wild Horses.

And thou, O *Phineus*[41]! why dost thou indulge that Jade *Harpalice* by digging out the Eyes of thy Children? Believe me, Divine Vengeance will hereafter inflict the same Punishment on thyself.

All these have been the Effects of Women's raging Desires, which are so much more violent and mad than ours.

Come on then, and doubt not the Conquest of any Girl whatever: there is not one in a thousand who will deny you.

And even those who will deny you, love to be put to the Question; if you are disappointed therefore, your Repulse will be attended with no Danger.

But why should you apprehend any Disappointment, when every new Amour pleases them, and they all hanker after the Lovers and Husbands of other Women?

This I am afraid is too natural in all things. The Corn in our Neighbour's Field seems always to flourish beyond our own, and we think our own Cow gives less Milk than his.

However, before you attack any Lady, make first sure of her Maid; for she will pave the Way to your Addresses.

If the Lady have many Females about her Person, take care to secure her who is most in the Confidence of her Mistress; and who will faithfully betray to you all her private Conversation.

When you have found this Confidant out, corrupt her with Promises and Intreaties; for she can soon bring you to the End of your Desires, if she pleases.

Let her watch the Opportunity, (Physicians will tell you the Use of attending proper Seasons) when the Mind of your Mistress is easy, and apt for your Purpose.

This Season, I apprehend, is when she is in the best Humour; for Love then becomes luxuriant in her Mind, as Corn doth in a rich Soil.

When the Heart is full of Gladness, and bound up by no Vexation,

it is open; and then the Compliments of a Lover will easily find an Admission.

Remember, *Troy* was defended while it remained in a sullen Mood, and opened its Gates to the armed Horse, when it was full of Good-Humour, and drunk with Joy.

Yet every Vexation should not deter you; for if your Mistress should be uneasy at the Falshood of her Husband, then is a proper time to attack her, and to assist her in revenging the Injury.

When your Mistress is in this Humour, let *Abigail* while combing her Hair at the Toilette in a Morning, stir her up to Vengeance. This will underhand promote your Voyage; for while you openly manage your Sails, she works under the Water with her Oars.

Now let Abigail with a soft Sigh mutter to her self: *Ah! poor Lady, I am afraid it is not in your power alone to revenge your Husband's Perfidy!*

Then let her introduce a Discourse of you; let her say something in your Favour, and swear that you are gone distracted and dying for Love.

But no Time must be lost; lest the Passions she hath raised should again subside; and Resentment intervene by Delay, and freeze up her Love as Ice doth Water.

And here perhaps you will ask a Question, Whether it is prudent to kiss the Agent herself. This is not easy to answer: for it is a mere Cast of the Dye, whether you succeed the better of the worse for it.

One Woman is by Enjoyment made a more industrious Solicitor, another becomes just the reverse. One thinks of procuring the Pleasures she hath tasted for her Mistress, another of securing them herself.

The Event is doubtful; and though she may be easy enough to be had, my Advice is, abstain from the Confidant; for I will not imitate the Empyric in striking bold Strokes; nor will I lead my Scholars over a Precipice. I give no Advice but what is safe, nor shall any Youth by following my Precepts run himself into *Rosamond's Pond.*

If therefore the Girl who goes between you and your Mistress, pleases you in her Person as well as in her Diligence; enjoy the Mistress first, and the Maid falls of course; but never begin with the latter.

One thing however I must admonish you, (if my Art deserves

any Credit, and my Words are to be regarded as any thing better than Wind) EITHER NEVER ATTEMPT THE CONFIDANT, OR GO THOROUGH STITCH WITH HER: for by making her *particeps criminis* you take away her Evidence.

This Doctrine you may learn from all other Sportsmen: for if a Bird escapes with Birdlime on his Wings, or a Boar breaks through the Toils, or a Fish gets off from the Hook; they are all sure to alarm their Companions, and spoil the Sport of the Fowler, the Hunter, or the Fisher. If once therefore you attempt her, press her to it with all your Vigour, and never leave her till you have enjoyed her.

For when once she is involved in the same Guilt with yourself, you are sure she will not betray you. Nay, you may be assured further, that she will betray every Word and Action of her Mistress to you.

But take particular care not to blab any of the Secrets she discloses to you: for while her Mistress hath no Suspicion of her Confidant, she will be able to lay her entirely open to your Knowledge.

And now, to resume that Matter, believe me, he is deceived, who thinks that none but the Farmer and Mariner are obliged to regard the Season: for as it is not proper at all times to commit the Corn to the fallacious Fields, nor to trust your Vessel at all times to the green Ocean; so neither is it always safe to attack a tender Girl, for she will be taken at one time who will resist at another. If it be for instance her Birth-day[42], perhaps, her Grandmother hath instructed her to be particularly cautious on that day; so if it be the Day of the Week on which *Childermas* hath happened to fall that Year; or King *Charles's* Martyrdom: defer the attack at all such Seasons. For to speak in Sea-Language, then is dirty Weather[43], then it blows a Hurricane; and if you weigh Anchor at that Season, you will be scarce able to keep your keel downwards.

Above all avoid your Mistress's Birth-day; nor will it be more prudent in you to visit her first on the Morning of *Valentine's* Day[44], you will pay more for being her Valentine than it is worth. Indeed all Seasons which give them any Hint of receiving Presents should be carefully avoided: for be never so cautious and sneaking, have it of you she will. They all very well know the Art of squeezing a Lover who longs to squeeze them.

Mr.[C] *Deards* will make his Appearance in his Silk Night-Gown, and unbundle his Packet in your Presence. The Lady will then desire

you to look over his Trinkets, (she can do no less, you know, in Compliment to your Taste:) then she will make you a Present of a Kiss, and afterwards desire you to buy it.

[Note C: An eminent Joyner in *London*.]

"I promise you, my Dear," says she, "if you will but buy me this single Jewel, I will not ask another of you the Lord knows how long; but I have really a present Occasion for this, and besides it is the cheapest Thing I ever saw."

If you pretend to have no Money about you, the Answer is, O, my Dear, you may give your Note: Mr. *Deards* will take your Note. So that you may repent having learnt to write your Name. Then she adds, *O la, I had almost forgot, it is my Birth-day, I am sure you will make me a Present on my Birth-day*: for they can be born every Day in the Year to serve their Purpose. Or else she pretends to have lost a Drop from her Ear-Ring; this Loss makes her miserable, and sure, says she, *if you loved me, you would repair that Loss*.

Nay, some are not so honest as to desire a Present, they only borrow; but they are sure never to restore. By this Means you lose the Thing, without having the Merit of bestowing it.

In short, if I had ten Mouths, with ten Tongues in each, all would not suffice to display all the Arts by which Harlots pick the Pockets of their Cullies.

Begin then your Amour with an Epistle; let that break the Ice for you, and make the first Discovery of your Flame.

In this you may insert all your little Blandishments, and Expressions of Fondness, nor be ashamed, however high your Quality is, to add the strongest Entreaties.

Remember that many a Rebel's Son hath had his Life spared at the Supplication of his Father; nay, the Wrath of Heaven itself is often averted by Prayer.

It is moreover my Advice to you, to be liberal of your Promises; for what Injury can you receive by Promising? This is a Treasure in which any Man may be rich.

Nor can your Mistress complain that she is absolutely cheated, if you can bring her to believe your Promises. A lifely Faith hath supported many a Man for a long Time: For though our Faith may sometimes deceive us, it is however a great and commodious Virtue.

Beware of giving: For when once your Mistress hath the Present in her Clutches, she may answer jilting you to her Prudence. She hath gained at least what she is in possession of, and cannot be said to have lost any thing by the Bargain.

On the contrary, keep her still in Expectation. Seem always about to give, but never part with a Shilling: For in this Manner doth a barren Soil often deceive its Owner. Thus, that he may not be a Loser, the Gamester pushes on his ill Luck, and one flattering Throw makes him eager to have the Box again in his Hands.

Indeed the great Business is to enjoy your Mistress before she hath touched you. If she once yield to you gratis, she will continue to bestow her Favours still gratis, in Hopes of being at last rewarded for all her past Favours.

Epistolize therefore first; flatter and sooth her with tender Lines. Let these probe her Mind, and open the Way for your Addresses.

You know the Story of *Cydippe*[45], who was outwitted by a Letter inclosed in an Apple; by which Means she was made to speak Words she never intended.

I would advise the young Gentlemen of the *Temple*, to study the Arts of Persuasion, on other Accounts, besides that of defending Sheep-stealers at an Assizes: For a pretty Girl may be as easily captivated by Eloquence, as a Judge or Jury; and surely she is a much nobler Prize.

But here conceal your Art, and do not carry your Eloquence in your Face: And above all Things, beware of hard Words; for who but an empty Coxcomb ever made a verbose Declamation to his Mistress? By such Methods you may raise her Abhorrence more probably than her Love.

Let your Passion appear credible, and disclose it in easy and common Language; it may be as tender and warm as you please; but preserve the Stile of Conversation.

If she should not receive your Letter, but send it back unopened, hope for better Success another Time, and maintain your Purpose.

Time brings the Stubborn Steer to bend his Neck to the Yoke, and the Horse to endure the Bridle.

Iron Bonds and Ploughshares are worn out by constant Use. What is harder than a Rock? or what is softer than Water? And yet hard Rocks are hollowed by soft Water.

Penelope herself in Time might have been conquered. You see *Troy*, though it defended itself so long, was however taken at last.

If she reads your Letters, but is unwilling to answer them, do not attempt to compel her. If she but reads your Fondness, it is sufficient.

If she will read, in Time she will answer what she reads. All these Matters will be brought about in their own good Time.

Perhaps the first Answer she sends you will be a cruel one, and may desire you to quit all future Solicitations.

She fears to be taken at her Word, and hopes you will not grant her Request. Follow her, and in Time you will obtain your Wishes.

If you meet her Chair, and the Curtains should be drawn, approach it as it were by Accident; and when you discover her there, whisper something tender in her Ear; but whisper softly, lest the Chairman, or any other impertinent Person, should over-hear you.

When she walks in the *Mall*, dangle after her, and interrupt her Walk with your Conversation.

Here you will have an Opportunity of seeing her Shape, and shewing her yours, by sometimes walking behind, and sometimes before her.

But for the most Part keep even pace with her, whether she trips along briskly, or only saunters.

Sometimes she will take a longer Walk, as far perhaps as the second or Third Stone. Hither follow her, and take every Opportunity of getting up close to her Side.

Never let her go to the Play without attending her: No Matter what the Play is, she will bring sufficient Entertainment for you with her.

Here keep your Eyes always intent on her only, and admire every Thing about her. By your Eyes, and by Signs, you may inform her of many Things.

Be sure to applaud greatly any amorous wanton Dance; and be no less favourable to those Scenes where the Business of Love is transacted, and almost brought to a Conclusion on the Stage: Many of which occur in *Congreve, Vanbrugh*, and *Wycherly*.

If she rises between the Acts, rise also; if she sits, as sometimes Ladies do, to express their Contempt for the Audience, do you likewise keep your Seat. In a Word, conduct yourself entirely according to her Example and Pleasure.

Now with regard to your Person: Do not imitate some finical *Petit Matre* in his *Toupet*, much less in more detestable Effeminacies.

Tuck your Hair rather under your Hat, like the rough Fox-hunter, who traverses Hill and Dale to the Musick of the Horn.

A careless Air in Dress becomes a Man. Colonel *Theseus*[46] carried off Miss *Ariadne* in a Campaign Wig without a single Curl in it.

In the same Manner did Captain *Hippolytus* march off with Miss *Phaedra*, though his Shock Head of Hair never had any Powder in it: nay, Lady *Venus* herself chose young *Jack Adonis* in a Jockey Coat and Buckskin Breeches.

Cleanliness however is agreeable: Let your Face be burnt with the Sun; but let your Cloaths be well made, and without a Spot on them.

Wash your Mouth, and clean your Teeth often; let your Beard be close shaved, and your Nails short and free from Dirt.

Observe these Documents, and leave all other Niceties to the Women, and to Men who desire to supply their Places.

But now *Bacchus* summons his Poet. He likewise assists Lovers, and favours the Flame which warms himself.

The *Cretan* Lady having jumped out of Bed in a raving Fit, wandered on the foreign Shore of *Dia*. She had nothing on but a loose wrapping Gown, without Stockings or Cap: and her Hair hung dishevelled over her Shoulders. She complained of the Cruelty of *Theseus* to the deep Waves, whilst an unworthy Shower of Tears ran down her Cheeks. She wept, and lamented aloud, and both became her; nor did her Tears diminish her Beauty. Once, and again, she beat her delicious Breasts with her Hands, and cried aloud, *The perfidious Man hath abandoned me; What will become of poor* Ariadne? *What will become of poor* Ariadne? On a sudden a vast Multitude was heard, while many Kinds of strange Instruments, like those of the miserable Masons, accompanied the Voices. The poor Lady sunk with Fear; and suppressed her last Words; nor did the least Blood remain in her Countenance. And now behold the *Bacchanalian* Women, with their Hair about their Ears, and the light Satyrs, who are always Forerunners of the God. Behold old Master *Silenus*[47] as drunk as a Piper, riding on an Ass, which he is hardly able either to sit or guide. The old Gentleman, endeavouring to follow the *Bacchanalians*, who fly from him and towards him, sets Spurs to his Ass, which being a vicious Beast, kicked up, and threw him over his Ears: upon which all the Satyrs set up a loud Shout, crying out, *Rise, Father, rise and be d——nd to you*. And now the God himself, high mounted on his Four-Wheel Chaise, the Top of which was adorned with Grapes, and which he drove himself, flung his Golden Reins over the Backs of his Pair of Tygers. Poor *Ariadne's* Colour forsook her Cheeks, and *Theseus* and her Voice at once deserted her Lips. Thrice she attempted to fly, and thrice being retained, she grew stiff

with Fear, and stood trembling as Corn waves in the Field, or Reeds on the River Bank, when fanned by the Wind. To whom the God; *Behold, Madam, a more faithful Lover at your Feet: Fear nothing, Lady fair, you shall be the Wife of* Bacchus. *The Sky shall be your Dowry, where shining in a bright Constellation, by the Name of* Ariadne's *Crown, you shall often direct the doubtful Mariner's Passage.* He said; and leaping from his Chariot, lest *Ariadne* should be afraid of the Tygers, the Sand sunk under the Weight of his Feet; and catching her instantly in his Arms, he carried her, who was incapable of scratching, directly off; (for every Thing, we know, is in the Power of a Deity:) And now, whilst Part of his Train sing the *Hymenaeum*, and other cry *Evie Evoe*, two very mysterious Words, and full of Masonry, the God and his new-ravished Bride go together, between a Pair of sacred Sheets.

Whenever therefore you happen to be in Company with a pretty Girl over a Bottle, pray heartily to *Bacchus*, and invoke his nocturnal Rites, that the Wine may not get into your Head. You may now take an Opportunity to toast some Nymph by a fictitious Name, of whom you may say an hundred amorous Things; all which, with the least Assistance, she will readily apply to herself. Double Entendres likewise may be used. You may moreover draw certain Figures in Wine on the Table; and after having spoken of your Mistress in the third Person, you may take this Method of writing her Name, and convincing her, that she herself is the Goddess.

But let your gloating Eyes inform her of your Passion: for an expressive Countenance often finds both Words and Utterance.

When she drinks, receive the Cup from her; and let her see you industrious to find out the Place before pressed by her Lips; and then drink eagerly at the same.

And whatever Part of the Meat she shall touch with her Fingers, do not fail to give the Preference to that: if in catching at it, you touch her Hand into the Bargain, it is the better.

But above all Things, let it be your Endeavour to please her Keeper, if she have any: For to make a Friend of him will be very useful to you both.

When you are at Table, let him be always helped first, and to the most elegant Tid-Bit; and when you drink together, offer him always the Place of Toast-maker; whether he be your Inferiour or your Equal, let him always choose before you, and be not ashamed to trowel him well over with Flattery.

It is a safe and common Way to deceive under Pretence of Friendship; I must own, however safe and common it is, it is not altogether blameless.

This is indeed a Dishonesty not very unlike that of a Major Domo, who under the Colour of Friendship empties your Cellars of your Wine, by pushing the Bottle further than is necessary.

Now to fix a certain Stint to your Cups, I allow you never to drink till your Head becomes giddy, and your Feet begin to totter.

Beware of Quarrels, which are often occasioned by Wine. Let not your Hands be too ready to strike in your Cups.

Remember the old Story of the Wedding of *Pyrothous*[48] and many more where drunken Fools by being quarrelsome in their Liquor have come short home. A Drinking Bout is in Reality a properer Scene for Joke and Mirth, than for Fighting.

I proceed to other Lessons[49]. If you have a Voice, then sing; if you have handsome Legs, cut Capers, or slide into the Minuet Step. In short, endeavour to please your Mistress, by exerting those Talents in which Nature hath given you to excel.

Now, as real Drunkenness may be hurtful to you, so you may sometimes reap Advantages by pretending yourself in Liquor, by Stammering or Lisping a little slyly: For then if you should descend to some Expressions of the grosser Kind, it will be imputed to your having taken a Cup too much.

Drink Bumpers to the Health of your Mistress, and of the Gentleman with whom she is obliged to sleep; but I do not insist on your being extremely sincere on this Occasion: for you may heartily wish him hanged at the same Time, if you please.

When the Company rises to go away, there is always a Confusion in the Room, of which you may take Advantage. You may then creep close up to your Mistress, may perhaps palm her, and gently tread on her Toes.

Whenever you have an Opportunity of speaking to her privately, be not bashful like a Country Boobily Squire. Remember Fortune and Love both favour the Bold.

I do not intend to lay down any Rules for your Oratory on this Occasion. Do but begin boldly, and you will be Eloquent of course: Set this only before you, that you are to act the Part of a Lover, to talk of Wounds and Darts, and Dying and Despair, and all that, as Mr. *Bayes* says: For if you can once make her believe you are in Love, your Business is done. To create therefore this Faith in her,

you must employ every Art of which you are Master.

Nor is this indeed so difficult a Task: For every Woman believes herself to be the Object of Love; be she never so ugly, she is still amiable in her own Eye.

Sometimes indeed no Deceit is in the End put on the Woman, for her pretended Lover becomes often a real one, and is the very Creature which he before personated.

And by the Way, young Ladies, let me tell you this is no small Encouragement to you, to countenance such Pretences; for if you manage well, you may often inspire a Man with Love in Earnest, while he is endeavouring to impose a fictitious Passion upon you.

But to return to my Scholars. Flatter with all your Might: for the Mind is taken as it were by Stealth, by Flattery, even as the Bank which hangs over a River is undermined by the liquid Waves.

Never be weary therefore of commending her Face, or her Hair; her taper Arm, or her pretty little Foot.

The chastest Matrons are fond of hearing the Praises of their Beauty; and the purest Virgins make the Charms of their Persons at once their Business and their Pleasure.

What else is meant by that ancient Fable of *Juno* and *Pallas*, whom the *Greek* Poets represent as yet ashamed of the Conquest obtained by *Venus*.

This Vanity seems to extend itself to Animals, in many of which we may observe some Traces of it.

The peacock, if you seem to admire her, spreads forth her Golden Plumes, which she never displays to an indifferent Spectator.

The Race-Horse, while he is running for a Plate, enjoys the Beauties of his well-combed Mane, and gracefully turned Neck.

Secondly, to Flattery, add Promises, and those not timorous nor sneaking ones. If a Girl insists upon a Promise of Marriage, give it her, and bind it by many Oaths[D]; for no Indictment lies for this sort of Perjury.

The Antients vented horrid Impieties on this Occasion, and introduced *Jupiter* shaking his Sides at the Perjuries of Lovers, and ordering the Winds to puff them away: Nay, he is said to have forsworn himself even by *Styx* to *Juno*: and therefore, say they, he encourages Men to follow his Example.

[Note D: This is the most exceptionable Passage in the whole Work. We have endeavoured to soften it as much as possible; but even as it now stands, we cannot help expressing Detestation of this Sentiment, which appears shocking even in a Heathen Writer.]

But though a Christian must not talk in this Manner, yet I believe it may be one of those Sins which the Church of *Rome* holds to be venial, or rather venal.

I would here by no Means be suspected of Infidelity or Profaneness. It is necessary there should be a God; and therefore we must believe there is; nay, we must worship him: For he doth not possess himself in that indolent State in which the Deities of *Epicurus* are depictured. If we live innocent Lives, we may depend on the Care of his Providence.

Restore faithfully whatever is deposited in your Hands: Be just in all your Contracts: Avoid all Kind of Fraud, and be not polluted with Blood. A wise Man will be a Rogue only among the Girls: For in all other Articles a Gentleman will be ashamed of breaking his Word.

And what is this more than deceiving the Deceivers? The Sex are for the greatest Part Impostors; let them therefore fall in the Snares which they have spread for others.

Perhaps you have never read the Justice of *Busiris*; when Egypt was burnt up Nine Years together for want of Rain, one *Thrasius* a Foreigner came to Court, and being introduced to the King by *Clementius Cotterelius*, he acquainted his Majesty, that *Jupiter* was to be propitiated by the Blood of a Stranger. The King Answered him, *Then thou thyself shalt be the first Victim, and with thy foreign Blood shalt give Rain to Egypt.*

To the same Purpose is the Story of *Phalaris*, who roasted the Limbs of *Perillus* in his own Bull: Thus making Proof of the Goodness of the Work by the Torments of the unhappy Maker.

Now there was great Justice in both these Examples; for nothing can be more equitable than that the Inventers of Cruelty should perish by their own Art.

To apply this to our present Purpose: As there is no Deceit or Perjury which Women will stick at putting in use against us, let them lament the Consequence of their own Examples.

Thirdly, Tears are of great Service. The Proverb tells you, *Tears will move Adamant*. If you can bring it about therefore, let your Mistress see your Cheeks a little blubbered upon Occasion.

If Tears should refuse to come (as they sometimes will) an Onion in your Handkerchief will be of great use.

Fourthly, Kisses. What Lover of any Sense doth not mix Kisses with his tender Expressions! Perhaps she will not give them easily:

No Matter, take them without her Leave.

Perhaps she will scratch, and say you are rude: Notwithstanding her Scratches, she will be pleased with your getting the better.

Do this, however, in so gentle a Manner, that you may not hurt her tender Lips; nor let her complain of being scrubbed with your Beard.

Now when you have proceeded to Kisses, if you proceed no farther, you may well be called unworthy of what you have hitherto obtained. When you was at her Lips, how near was you to your Journey's End! If therefore you stop there, you rather deserve the Name of a bashful 'Squire than of a modest Man.

The Girls may call this perhaps Violence; but it is a Violence agreeable to them: For they are often desirous of being pleased against their Will: For a Woman taken without her Consent, notwithstanding her Frowns, is often well satisfied in her Heart, and your Impudence is taken as a Favour; whilst she who, when inclined to be ravished, hath retreated untouched, however she may affect to smile, is in reality out of Humour.

Ravishing is indeed out of Fashion in this Age; and therefore I am at a Loss for modern Examples; but antient Story abounds with them.

Miss[50] *Phoebe* and her Sister were both ravished, and both were well pleased with the Men who ravished them.

Though the Story of *Deidamia* was formerly in all the *Trojan* News-Papers, yet my Reader may be pleased to see it better told.

Venus had now kept her Word to *Paris*, and given him the Beauty she had promised, not as a Bribe, but as a Gratification for his having made an Award in her Favour, in the famous Cause between *Juno* and others against *Venus*, in *Trover* for a Golden Apple; which was referred to him at the Assizes at *Ida*.

Paris, every one knows, no sooner had received Mrs. *Helen*, than he immediately carried her off to his Father's Court.

Upon this the *Grecians* entered into an Association; and several Noblemen raised Regiments at their own Expence, out of their Regard to the Public: For Cuckoldom was a public Cause, no one knowing whose Turn it would be next.

Lieutenant-General *Achilles*, who was to command a large Body of Grenadiers, which the *Greeks* call *Myrmidons*, did not behave handsomely on that Occasion, though he got off afterwards at a Court-Martial by pleading, that his Mother (who had a great deal in her own

Power) had insisted on his acting the Part he did; for, I am ashamed to say, he dressed himself in Women's Clothes, and hid himself at the House of one *Lycomedes*, a Man of good Fortune in those parts.

Fie upon it, General, I am ashamed to see you sit quilting among the Girls; a Sword becomes your Hands much better than a Needle.

What can you mean by that Work-Basket in a Hand by which Count Hector *is to fall? Do you carry that Basket with you to put his Head in?*

For Shame then, cast away your Huswife, and all those effeminate Trinkets from a Fist able to wield Harry *the Fifth's Sword.*

It happened, that at the same Time when the General, at the House of 'Squire *Lycomedes*, performed this Feat, Miss *Deidamia*, one of the Maids of Honour, was visiting at the same Place. This young Lady soon discovered that the General was a Man; for indeed he got her Maidenhead.

He ravished her, that is the Truth on't; that a Gentleman ought to believe, in Favour of the Lady: But he may believe the Lady was willing enough to be ravished at the same Time.

When the General threw away his Needle, and grasped the Armour, (you must remember the Story, for it was in the *Trojan Alamain*) the young Lady began to change her Note, and to hope he would not forsake her so.

Ah! little Mia! *is this the Violence you complained of? Is this the Ravisher you are afraid of? Why with that gentle Voice do you solicite the Author of your Dishonour to stay with you?*

To come at once to the Moral of my Story; as they are ashamed to make the first Advances, so they are ready to suffer whatever a pushing Man can do unto them.

As for those pretty Master-Misses, the *Adonis's* of the Age, who confide in their own Charms, and desire to be courted by the Girls; believe me, they will stay long enough before they are asked the Question.

If you are a Man, make the first Overtures: Remember, it is the Man's Part to address the Fair; and it will be her's to be tenderly won.

Be bold then, and put the Question; she desires no more than to have the Question put; and sure you will not deny your own Wishes that Favour.

Jupiter himself went a courting to the Heroines of old: For I never heard of any Girl who courted him.

But if you find Madam gives herself any immoderate Airs at your Proposal, it will then be good to recede a little from your Undertaking, and to affect to sheer off: For many of them, according to the Poet,

Pursue what flies, and fly what doth pursue.

A short Absence will soon cure her Disdain.

It may be proper likewise to conceal your intentions a little at first, and make your first Advance under the Pretence of *Platonic* Friendship.

I have known many a Prude taken under these false Colours; and the *Platonic* Friend hath soon become a happy Lover.

And now as to your Complexion; for believe me, this is a Matter of some Consequence: Though I would not have you effeminate, yet I would have you delicate.

A fair Complexion in a Tar is scandalous, and looks more like a Borough Captain or one of those fresh-water Sailors, who have so much dishonoured our Navy. The Skin of a Seaman ought to be rough, and well battered with Winds and Waves.

Such likewise ought to be the Face of a Fox-hunter, who ought not to fear Rain or Easterly Winds: And the fame becomes the Soldier.

But let the Soldier of *Venus* look fair and delicate; nay, if your Complexion inclines to Paleness, so much the better; for this will be imputed by every young Girl to Love.

Young *Orion*[51] with a pale Countenance wandered through the Groves, being sick with the Love of Lyrice: And the same Effect had the Love of *Naïs* upon the Countenance of *Daphnis*[52]; two Lovers very famous in Antiquity.

Leanness is another Token of a Lover; to obtain which, you need not take Physick; sitting up all Night; and writing Love-Letters, will bring this about.

Be sure to look as miserable as possible; so that every one who sees you, may cry, *There goes a Lover*.

And here shall I lament the Wickedness of Mankind, or only simply observe it to you? But in Reality all Friendship and Integrity are nothing more than Names.

Alas! It is dangerous to be too prodigal in the Praises of your Mistress, even to your Friend; for if he believes you, he becomes your Rival.

It is true there are some old Stories of faithful Friends: *Patroclus* never made a Cuckold of *Achilles*; and *Phaedra's* Chastity was never attempted by *Pirithous*.

Pylades loved *Hermions*, who was his Friend's Wife; but it was with the pure Love of a Brother: And the same Fidelity did *Castor* preserve towards his Twin-Brother *Pollux*.

But if you expect to find such Instances in these degenerate Days, you may as well have Faith enough to expect a Pine-Apple from a Pear-Tree, or to hope to fill your Bottle with *Burgundy* from the River.

I am afraid we are grown so bad, that Iniquity itself gives a Relish to our Pleasures; and every Man is not only addicted to his Pleasures, but those are the sweeter, when season'd with another's Pain.

It is in short a terrible Case, that a Lover ought to fear his Friend more than his Enemy. Beware of the former, and you are safe.

Beware of your Cousin, and your Brother, and your dear and intimate Companions. These are the Sort of Gentry, from whom you are to apprehend most Danger.

Here I intended to have finished; but one Rule more suggests itself.

You are to note then, that there is a great Variety in the Tempers of Women; for a thousand different Women are to be wooed a thousand different Ways.

Mr. *Miller* will tell you, that the same kind of Soil is not proper for all Fruits. One produces good Carrots, another Potatoes, and a third Turneps. Now there is as great a Variety of Disposition in the human Mind, as there are Forms in the World: For which Reason a Politician is capable of accommodating himself to innumerable Kinds of Tempers: Not *Proteus* could indeed diversify himself more Ways than he can.

Nay you may learn this Lesson from every Fisherman; for some Fish are to be taken with one Bait, and some with another; others will scarce bite at any, but are however to be drawn out of the Water by a Net.

One good Caution under this Head, is to consider the Age of your Mistress: Old Birds are not taken with Chaff; and an old Hare will be sure to double.

Again, consider Circumstances. Do not frighten an ignorant Woman with Learning, nor a poor Country Girl with your fine Cloathes;

for by these Means you will create in them too great an Awe of you. Many a Girl hath run away frighted from the Embraces of the Master, and afterwards fallen into the Clutches of his Footman.

And here we will now cast our Anchor, having finished the first Part of our intended Voyage.

FINIS

FOOTNOTES

[1] Here *Ovid* uses the Examples of *Automedon*, who was the Coachman of *Achilles*; and of *Tiphys*, who was Pilot or Steersman to the *Argonauts*.

[2] This is a literal Translation; by which it appears this barbarous Custom of whipping Boys on the Hands, till they look as if they had the Itch, was used by the *Roman* Schoolmasters as well as by ours.

[3] The Original introduces *Achilles*, who was the pupil of *Chiron*.

[4] In the Original,—*held forth at his Master's Commands those Hands to be whipt, which* Hector *was hereafter to feel*. The Indelicacy of which Image we have avoided applying to our *British* Hero.

[5] *Both born of a Goddess.*

[6] This is transferred, we hope not improperly from *Roman* to *British* Superstition. The *Latin* alludes to Augury, and very justly ridicules the Folly of Divination by the Flight of Birds.

[7] *Nor were* Clio *or her Sisters seen by me, while I tended a Flock in the Valleys of Ascra.* This *Ascra* was a Valley near the *Helicon*, which was the Residence of the Parents of *Hesiod*. Now *Hesiod* was fabled, whilst he was keeping his Father's Sheep, to have been led by the Muse to the Fountain *Hippocrene*; and being, I suppose, well ducked in that Water, commenced Poet.

[8] This whole Passage is a manifest Burlesque on the Invocations with which the Ancients began their Poems. Not very different is that Sneer at the Beginning of the *Metamorphosis*,

—— *Dii, caeptis*, (NAM VOS MUTASTIS ET ILLAS) *Adspirate* ——

But the strongest Piece of Burlesque of this kind is the Invocation to *Venus* at the Beginning of *Lucretius*: For what can be more so than a solemn Application to a Deity for her Assistance in a Work, the professed Intention of which is to expose the Belief of any Deity at all; and more particularly of any Concern which such superior Beings might be supposed to take in the Affairs of Men. For my own part, I must confess, I cannot perceive *that graceful Air of Enthusiasm* which a noble Author observes in the Invocation of the Antients; many of them indeed seem to have been too apparently in jest, to endeavour to impose on their Readers, and in reality to apply to the Muses with less Devotion than our modern Poets, many of whom perhaps believe as much in those Deities as in any other.

[9] *Ovid* would here insinuate, that the Courtezans only were the Subjects of the ensuing Poem; and in his *Tristibus* he cites these Lines, and pleads them in his Defence: But he is not over-honest in his Profession; for in many Parts it appears, that his Instructions are calculated for much more than *concessa furtia.*

[10] *Andromeda* was the Daughter of *Cepheus* King of *Aethiopia* and of *Cassiope.* Her Mother having offended the *Nereids*, by contending with them for Superiority in Beauty, *Neptune*, at their Petition, sent a Sea-Monster, which greatly annoyed the *Aethiopians.* Upon this they consulted the Oracle of *Jupiter Ammon*, who ordered them to expose one of the Progeny of *Cepheus* and *Cassiope* to be devoured by the Monster. *Andromeda* was accordingly ty'd to a Rock, where she was espied by *Perseus*, who killed the Monster, and rescued the Lady; for which he received her at the Hands of her Parents as his Reward. The Story is told in the 4th Book of the *Metamorphosis.*

[11] *Bunches of Grapes in* Methymna; a City of *Lesbia*, the Wine of which Country was famous among the Ancients.

[12] *Ears of Corn in* Gargara; which was in *Mysia*, a Province of the *Hellespont.*

[13] The Original is, *And the Mother of* AEneas *resides in the City of her Son. AEneas*, from whom the Romans derived their Original, was the Son of *Venus* by *Anchises.*

[14] The Original, rendered as literally as possible, is as follows: *Walk at your ease under the* Pompeian *Shade, when the Sun enters the* Herculean *Lion; or where the Mother hath added her Benefactions to those of her Son; a work rich in foreign Marble: Nor avoid that Portico adorned with*

ancient Pictures, which is called Livia, *from the Name of its Founder: nor that adorned by the Statues of the* Belides, *who attempted the Lives of their unfortunate Cousins; and where you see the cruel Father standing with his drawn Sword: Nor pass by the Temple of* Venus *and her lamented* Adonis; *nor omit the Seventh-Day Festivals of the* Jews; *nor the* Egyptian *Temples of the* Linnen-clad *Heifer: She makes many Women to be that which she herself was to* Jupiter.

To explain these several Particulars to an *English* Reader, it must be known, that the Portico's in *Rome* were the publick Walks; and here Persons of both Sexes used to assemble. Among these was one built by *Pompey.* The second Portico mentioned, is by the best Commentators understood of the *Octavian,* which was built by *Octavia,* Sister to *Augustus,* and Mother to *Marcellus*; and this adjoined to a Temple built by the same *Marcellus.* The third Portico was built by *Livia* the Wife of *Augustus,* and called from her Name. The fourth, where the Picture of the *Belides* was, is to be understood of the Portico of *Apollo Palatinus,* in which were the Statues of the fifty Daughters of *Danaus* and Grandaughters of *Belus.* These being married to the fifty Sons of their Uncle *AEgyptus,* every one, by her Father's Command, slew her husband on the first Night, save only *Hypermnestra.* For this they were punished in the lower World, by being obliged to fill a Barrel full of Holes with Water. *Scaliger* and others have here made a mistake, supposing the Picture of the *Belides* was here hung up: But the contrary appears by many Authorities, particularly by this in *Qv. Trist. 3.*

Signa peregrinis ubi sunt alterna columnis, Belides, & stricto barbarus ense pater.

It appears that the Number of Pillars was equalled by the Number of Statues.

5thly, The Temple of *Venus,* in which she was worshipped, together with *Adonis,* after the *Assyrian* manner. This *Adonis* was the Son of *Cinyras* King of *Cyprus,* begotten by him on his own Daughter *Myrrha.* The Fame of his Beauty, and the Passion which *Venus* bore towards him, are well known. 6thly, The *Jewish* Synagogues. The *Jews* having been encouraged by *Julius Caesar,* were very numerous in *Rome* at that time; and the Strangeness and Pomp of their Ceremonies inviting the Curiosity of the

Roman Ladies, their Synagogues became famous Places of Intrigue. 7. The Temple of *Isis*. This Goddess, when a Woman, was called *Io*. She was the Daughter of *Inachus*; and being beloved by *Jupiter*, was by him, to preserve her from his Wife's Jealousy, turned into a Heifer, *Juno* suspecting the Fact, obtained this Heifer of her Husband, and set Argus to watch over her. *Jupiter* wanting to visit his old Friend, sent *Mercury* to kill *Argus*; in revenge of which, *Juno* ordered a Gad-Bee to sting the poor Heifer; which thereupon growing mad, ran to *Egypt*, where she was again restored to the Shape of a Woman, and married to *Osiris*. The Feast of *Isis* was celebrated in *Rome* ten Days together by the Women, and was a time of Carnival among them.

[15] In *Caesar's Forum*, which was built on the *Appian* Way, was the Temple of *Venus Genetrix*.

[16] Races were run at *Rome* in *April* in the *Circus Maximus*, which was likewise the Scene of many other public Exercises and Shews.

[17] *And when the Procession shall pass on with the Ivory Deities, do you applaud most the Statue of* Lady *Venus.* Thus the Original. The Paraphrase preserves the same Sense, though in other Circumstances. These Statues were carried in Procession on many Occasions, particularly at the *Maegalesian* Games.

[18] *Adjusting her cushion.*

[19] *Putting a Foot-stool under her.*

[20] The Original mentioned the Fights of the *Gladiators*. The Paraphrase comes as near as our Customs admit; for the *British* Ladies never attend to see Men kill one another in jest.

[21] *Augustus Caesar* among other rich Shews, with which he entertained the People, exhibited to them a Sea-Fight in a Place dug on purpose near the banks of the *Tyber*. The Poet takes this occasion of introducing many Compliments to the Grandson of this Prince. We have done little more than altered Names in this Place; and as we are assured all here said is as properly applicable to the noble Person to whom we have transferred it, the learned Reader will admire that any Passage in an antient Author can

be so apposite to the present Times, and the true *English* Reader will be no less delighted to see *Ovid* introduced as singing forth the Praises of the *British Hero.*

[22] *Parthia.*

[23] The *Crassi.*

[24] *Hercules.*

[25] *Bacchus.*

[26] The Original here described the many Nations who are led Captives.

[27] Here we have inverted the Original; but sure the Sense upholds us in so doing.

[28] *Baiae*, a Place not far from *Naples*, famous for wholesome as well as pleasant Baths. It is described very largely by *Diodorus*; and *Horace* mentions it as the pleasantest Place in the World.

[29] In the Original, the Temple of *Diana* in the Suburbs. It stood in a Grove not far from Rome. The next Line, *Partaque per gladios, &c.* alludes to a very singular Custom, by which the Priests of this Temple succeeded to each other, *viz.* by Conquest in single Combat, for which every Slave or Fugitive was admitted to contend, and the Victor was rewarded with the Priesthood. This Practice was renewed every Year, and was, as *Strabo* informs us, originally taken from the *Scythians.*

[30] *Byblis* fell in love with her Brother *Caunus*; and upon his rejecting her Addresses, hanged herself. The Poets feign she was afterwards turned into a Fountain. See *Metam.* IX.

[31] *Myrrha* was the Daughter of *Cinyras*, who being in love with her Father, took an Opportunity, while her Mother was employed in the Sacrifices to *Ceres*, to supply her Place. Her Father discovering the Imposture, ran after her with a drawn Sword to kill her: But she escaped by means of the Night, and fled into *Sabeaea.* She was changed into the

Myrrh-Tree. The Story of which is in *Metam.* X. But though the Poets have subjoined Fable to this Fact, it is related by *Pliny* as a true History.

[32] *Pasiphaë* was the Daughter of the Sun, married to *Minos* King of *Crete.* The Poets feign that being in love with a Bull, she employed *Daedalus*, a famous Artist, to make her a wooden Cow, into which she conveyed herself, in order to enjoy her monstrous Desires. From this unnatural Coition sprung the *Minotaur*, a Monster half Man and half Bull, which was enclosed in a Labyrinth, and afterward destroyed by *Theseus.*

[33] The Original alludes to the *Cretans*, who were famous among the Antients for the Vice of lying.

[34] *Europa* was the Daughter of *Agenor* King of *Cydon*, beloved by *Jupiter*, and by him run away with in the Shape of a Bull.

[35] *AErope* was the Wife of *Atreus*. She committed Adultery with her Husband's Brother *Thyestes*, by whom she had two Sons, whom *Atreus* caused to be killed, and served up to his Brother's Table. To avoid this Sight, the Sun is said to have gone backward.

[36] *Scylla* the Daughter of *Nisus*, King of the *Megarensians*, fell in love with *Minos*, while he was besieging her Father's City. She stole away her Father's Hair, on which the Fate of the City depended, and carried it to *Minos*; for which Fact she was rewarded by her Lover with Contempt only.

She is by some said to have been changed into a Lark: But *Ovid*, who here seems to confound two Stories together, makes her Transformation to have been into a Rock, which lies between *Sicily* and *Italy*; where the dashing of the Waves against the Rock representing the Sound of the Barking of Dogs, gave rise to the Fable which is here hinted at.

[37] *Clytemnestra*, the Wife of *Agamemnon*, who in the absence of her Husband committed Adultery with *AEgysthus*, and with him afterwards murdered *Agamemnon*, at his Return from *Troy*.

[38] *Creüsa* was the Daughter of *Creon* King of *Corinth*, and second Wife to *Jason*; to whom *Medea*, enraged with *Jason*, who had forsaken her, sent a Casket in which Wild-Fire was inclosed, and by which she was burnt as

soon [as] it was opened. This *Medea* afterwards, on account of the same Anger with *Jason*, tore to pieces her two Sons which she had bore to him.

[39] This *Phoenix* having incensed his Father, by lying with a Woman who was beloved by the latter, fled to the Protection of *Peleus* the Father of *Achilles*, and was by bim [*sic*] Preceptor of that young Hero.

[40] *Hippolytus* being beloved by his Stepmother *Phaedra*, and refusing to gratify her Desires, was by her falsely accused to his Father *Theseus*; upon which account he was obliged to fly, and the Chariot Horses being frighted by Sea-Calves, dashed the Chariot to-pieces, and him also.

[41] *Phineus* King of *Arcadia*, having repudiated his Wife *Cleopatra*, married *Harpalice*; by whose Instigation he put out the Eyes of his Sons: for which he was afterwards punished by Divine Vengeance with the Loss of his own.

[42] The *Romans* paid a Religious Regard to their Birth-Day, as appears from many Passages in their Poets. At this time they used to receive Presents from their Relations and Acquaintance. We have here given the Sense of the Original, only varying the Customs (*Kalendae Martii*.) *Ovid* advises the Lover to abstain from visiting his Mistress in the Kalends of *March*. At which time the *Matronalia* were celebrated to *Juno Lucina*, and the Husbands used to pray to that Goddess to protect the Chastity of their Wives. *Horace* likewise Lib. III. Ode 8. hints that this was not the proper Season for Batchelors to give a Loose to their Gaieties. (*Sive erit ornatus Circus*, &c.) A third Caution *Ovid* gives, is not to visit on those Days when the Wealth of the *Roman* Conquests were exposed to the *Circus*, in admiring which, as *Mycellus* observes, the Girls were too much taken up, to attend to the Desires of their Lovers. To say the truth, some Custom seems to be alluded to here, which is not sufficiently preserved from the Ruins of Antiquity.

[43] *Then the* Pleiades *are at hand. Then the Goat is merged in the Sea*, *viz.* in the Month of *October* and *November*.

[44] The Original points at the Day in which the *Romans* were overthrown by the *Gauls* on the Banks of the River *Allia*. This was the 15th of the Kalends of *August*. A. U. C. 363, and it was marked as a black Day

in their Kalendar. As this Nation is too happy to produce any such Day, we have been obliged to give it a different Turn in our Paraphrase.

[45] *Cydippe* was a beautiful virgin of the island of *Delos*. She was celebrating the Rites of *Diana* when she was seen by *Acontius*, who falling in love with her, and not daring openly to declare his Passion, contrived to drop an Apple at her Feet, in which were inclosed these two Lines:

I swear to you by the mystical Rites of Diana, *That I will attend you as a Companion, and become your Bride.*

Cydippe took up the Apple and read the Lines; by repeating which words they became her own; and she was ignorantly betrothed to her Lover: For it was a Law, that whatever any persons said in *Diana's* Temple, they were obliged to perform.

[46] *Ariadne* was the Daughter of *Minos* King of *Crete*. She fell in Love with *Theseus*, and with a Clew of Thread helped him out of the Labyrinth into which he went to kill the *Minotaur*. He afterwards basely deserted the poor Lady, of which our Poet will presently tell the Story.

[47] *Silenus* was the Pedagogue of *Bacchus*, and his Foster-Father: He was likewise his Companion on all Occasions; and is often introduced in his drunken Mood by our Poet.

[48] At this Wedding *Eurytion* the *Centaur* getting drunk, attempted to ravish *Hippodamia* the Bride of *Pyrithous*, but *Theseus* knocked his Brains out with a Bowl. Upon this a Battle ensued between the *Centaurs* and the *Lapithae*, who defending the Cause of their Prince *Pyrithous*, destroyed almost all the *Centaurs*. *Horace* Lib. I. Ode 18. mentions this Story likewise, as a Caution to Men not to be quarrelsome in their Cups.

[49] Here and in many other Places, we have been obliged to supply that Connection, which is greatly wanting in the Original.

[50] *Phoebe* and *Ilaira* were two pretty Girls, the Daughters of *Leucippus*, and by their Father betrothed to two Brothers *Idas* and *Lynceus*; but before the Celebration of their Nuptials, were ravished by *Castor* and *Pollux*. This ended in the Death of *Castor*, by the Hands of *Lynceus*; and of *Lynceus*,

by *Pollux*, whose Death while *Idas* was attempting to revenge, he was struck dead by Thunder at the Feet of *Pollux*.

[51] *Orion* the *Theban* was in Love with *Merope* the Daughter of *AEnopian*; but who this *Lyrice* was, is not so plain, no Mention being made of her in any other Place.

[52] *Daphnis* was the Son of *Mercury*; for his Love for this *Naïs*, we have here *Ovid*'s Authority.